NO KISSES, PLEASE!

ISBN-13: 978-0-545-09891-5
ISBN-10: 0-545-09891-2

10 9 8 7 6 5 4 3   9 10 11 12 13/0

Printed in the U.S.A.
This edition first printing, January 2009

BEGINNING READER
LEVEL 1
50-250 WORDS

NO KISSES, PLEASE!

by Hans Wilhelm

SCHOLASTIC INC.

New York Toronto London Auckland Sydney

Mexico City New Delhi Hong Kong Buenos Aires

I hear a car!
We have a visitor.

Who can it be?

Oh, no.

It's Auntie Judy!

She always kisses me.

I hate kisses.
I must hide.

Now I am safe.

There you are.

I found you!

Oh, no!

HELLLLLP!

What should I do?

I have an idea!

I dig a hole.

Now you can kiss me.

It worked!
No kisses.

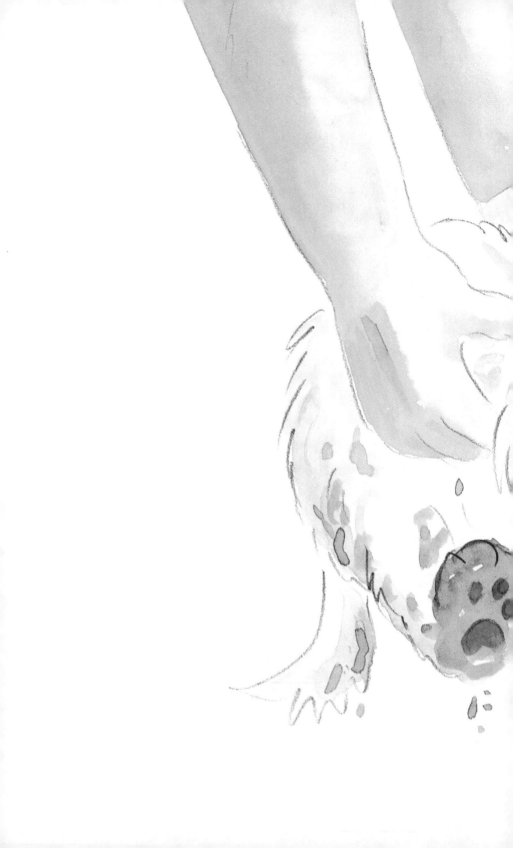

Oh, no. What now?

Baths are better than kisses.